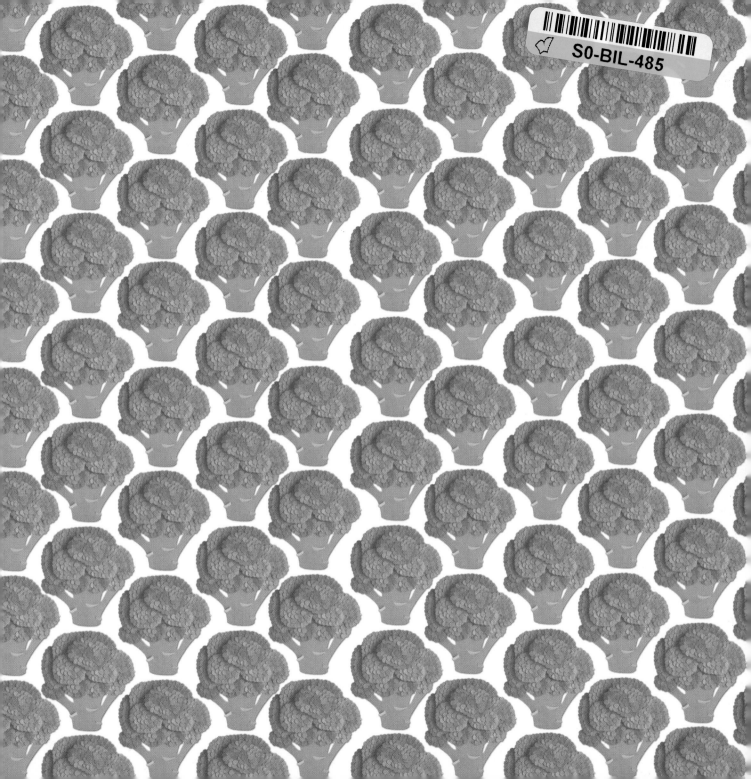

Bob's Booger

www.broccolipress.com

ISBN-10: 0-9850291-0-2
ISBN-13: 978-0-9850291-0-4

Library of Congress Control Number: 2012931517

The text is set in American Typewriter Regular.
The illustrations are rendered with cut paper.

Printed in Indianapolis

Broccoli
Press

Bob's Booger

by Scott Black

illustrated by Margaret TerBush

Bob was a kid 'bout nine years old.
And like kids do, Bob suffered from a cold.
All through the night, he snotted and he sneezed.
He didn't sleep a wink and he wasn't too pleased.

He wanted to stay home, but his mom said, "No way!"
So he had to get up for another school day!
He ate soggy flakes and he slurped pulpy juice.
He pulled on a sweater and he tied up his shoes.

He ran a comb through his hair and he pulled up his socks.
He grabbed his book bag and a rusty lunchbox.
He threw on his coat and he trudged toward the door,
With his head sort of achy and his throat kind of sore.

In the midst of his wheezing, two things he forgot:
Some cough drops for sucking and some tissues for snot.

Bob stood on the corner and waited for the bus
With a booger in his nose and his hair still a muss.
At the corner bus stop, the kids circled 'round Bob.
They pointed and they laughed and called him a slob.
Some kids cried, "Ewwww!" Others shrieked, "Gross!"
But none of them told 'im, he had a booger in his nose.

Bob boarded the bus to find a space,
But with each empty seat, he met a grimaced face.
He looked for his friend, but Joe wasn't around.
So he found an empty seat and plopped his bag to the ground.
As he sat on the bus, kids stared and they gawked.
Some looked away and other kids squawked.

When he got to school, he strolled down the hallway.
The kids whispered to each other and they started to say,
"Look at Bob's nose! Have you seen that thing?"
"It looks like a bell that's about to ring!"
"It's just hanging in there like a monkey in a tree."
"Will anyone tell him?"
"No, not me!"

So through all of his classes, from Art to Gym,
No one had the heart to tell him . . .

That he had a booger in his nose, which jiggled about.
It hung from his nostril, but it never fell out!

Then Bob's teacher called him over to the dusty chalkboard.
She needed his help, so she implored,
"Your good buddy, Joe, is at home sick,
He needs his homework; can you do the trick?
Take it to his house, 'cause he needs to get it done.
Tell him to bring it back, when his nose stops to run."
Then she looked at his nose and saw a green, crusty curd,
But she turned her head away and she didn't say a word.

On the bus ride home, with an armful of books,
Bob sat there and pondered why he got the strange looks.
But before he went home, he had one place to go.
He had to get the books to his good buddy, Joe.

Bob climbed up the steps and rang the doorbell.
Joe answered the door, but didn't look so well.
He wasn't too thrilled about the mountain of work,
But he thanked Bob kindly; he didn't want to be a jerk.

Just as Bob said, "You're welcome," and began to turn away,
Joe cleared his throat; he had something to say.
"Dude . . . I don't mean to be rude and I don't mean to be gross,
but just so you know, you've got a booger in your nose."

With a finger to his nostril, Bob plucked it out quick.
Then he turned away from Joe and he tossed it with a flick.
"Thanks, Dude."

It was at that moment on that particular day,
Bob learned a lesson that would never go astray.
In a world full of friends and a world full of foes,
A true friend will tell you . . . if you have a booger in your nose!